Layne the Surfing Fairy

By Daisy Meadows

ORCHARD

www.orchardseriesbooks.co.uk

Fairyland Palace
Surfing Festival
Port Pearl Beach
Skate Park
Youth Hostel

Jack Frost's Ice Castle

Goblin Grotto

Mistfall Mountains

Silverlake Valley

Dewbelle Ski Resort

Jack Frost's Ode

Each goody-goody fairy pest
Says 'Never cheat' and 'Try your best'.
Their words should end up in the bin.
To be the best you have to win!

I'll steal and cheat to find a way
Of winning every game I play,
And when the world is at my feet
They'll see it's always best to cheat!

Layne
the Surfing
Fairy

To Evie Dennett, who loves the fairies

Aberdeenshire Council Libraries	
4022148	
Askews & Holts	17-Jun-2021
JF	£4.99
J	

First published in Great Britain in 2021 by The Watts Publishing Group

1 3 5 7 9 10 8 6 4 2

A CIP catalogue record for this book is available from the British Library.

ISBN 978 1 40836 446 8

Printed and bound in Great Britain by Clays Ltd, Elcograf S.p.A

MIX
Paper from
responsible sources
FSC® C104740

The paper and board used in this book are made from wood from responsible sources.

Orchard Books
An imprint of Hachette Children's Group
Part of The Watts Publishing Group Limited
Carmelite House, 50 Victoria Embankment, London EC4Y 0DZ

An Hachette UK Company
www.hachette.co.uk
www.hachettechildrens.co.uk

Contents

Chapter One
The Games Begin

"Kirsty!" called Rachel Walker, waving madly from across Port Pearl Beach.

Her best friend, Kirsty Tate, let out a squeal of excitement. The girls tore across the silvery sand and flung their arms around each other.

"This is going to be amazing," said

Rachel, as soon as she got her breath back.

"I'm scared and excited at the same time," said Kirsty, jigging up and down.

"Me too," said Rachel. "I feel as if I've eaten ten bags of popping candy."

They held hands and looked around in awe. The beach was bustling with surfers, TV cameras and newspaper photographers. Food stalls filled the

air with yummy smells, and music was blasting out from the beach hut café in the sand dunes. Nearby, a TV reporter held up a microphone and smiled into her camera.

"It's day one of the School Gold Medal Games, and the competitors are eager to get started," she said. "Children have flocked to Port Pearl from all around the country to take part in our biggest sporting competition for schoolchildren."

"I'm so happy that our schools joined in," said Kirsty. "We get to take part in the competition together."

The girls had met on holiday, when they had helped to rescue the Rainbow Fairies. Since then, they had made friends with many fairies and shared lots of magical adventures.

"This year, the Gold Medal sports are surfing, skating, skiing and snowboarding," the reporter went on. "These beginner surfers are ready to catch some waves. The aim of the competition is to get children involved in sports they have never tried before, so everyone has an equal chance of winning. There's a great atmosphere here this morning. It feels more like a party than a competition!"

"Today is going to be brilliant," squealed Kirsty. "I hope my school wins one of the medals."

All around them, the competitors were pulling on wetsuits, checking their surfboards and making new friends. Rachel introduced Kirsty to one of her classmates.

"This is Shanti Sharma," she said. "We're all hoping that she's going to win a medal for Tippington School because she's picked up surfing so quickly. Shanti, this is my friend Kirsty."

"I am sure that there are loads of amazing surfers here," said Shanti. "It's great to meet you, Kirsty."

The music stopped, and a microphone whined as it was turned on. Everyone turned to the raised wooden stage at the top of the beach. A young woman waved to the crowd and then tapped her microphone.

"Hello and welcome to Port Pearl!" she called out. "I'm Kensa Lane, and I'm the head of the organising committee for the surfing championships. Wow, it's awesome to see so many people here today. Surfing brings out the best in me, and I feel sure it will do the same for all the budding surfers in the competition today."

There were whoops and cheers from the crowd, and Kensa grinned.

"One of the things I love about this sport is how it teaches everyone to be open-minded, care for others, seek out new challenges and not to take things too seriously," she said. "So let's have fun! Every surfer will take part in two heats and each heat will last twenty minutes."

"What's a heat?" asked Rachel.

"It's one round of the competition,"

Shanti explained. "They usually send about four surfers into the water at the same time."

"Catch as many waves as you can," said Kensa. "The longer you surf the wave, the higher your marks will be. Your top two scores will be placed on the leaderboard. At the end of the competition, the two highest scorers will have one final competition to win the gold medal. Let's get started!"

She pointed at the beach café and the music began to play again. There was a bustle of activity as the reporters chattered into their cameras.

"It's been so cool learning how to surf this summer," said Kirsty. "I fell off a *lot*."

"So did I," said Rachel with a giggle. "I don't think Shanti lost her balance once."

"Let's go and have a last practice now, while the judges are setting up," said Kirsty.

"I can't," said Shanti. "I've still got to pick up my competition number, but I'll see you later. Good luck!"

Rachel and Kirsty collected their surfboards and headed down to the shore. They checked for the lifeguards' flags to make sure they were safely between them, and then paddled out. Flecks of sunlight danced on the cool, clear water,

and the music faded into the background.

"Wow, the light is amazingly bright over there," said Rachel, sitting up on her board and shading her eyes with her hand.

"It's as if the sea is glowing," said Kirsty in an excited voice. "Rachel, I don't think that's sunlight. I think it's magic!"

Chapter Two
Festival in Fairyland

In the middle of the glowing patch of water, a fairy was floating on a tiny surfboard, her legs dangling in the water. Her shoulder-length brown hair was damp, and her blue eyes sparkled when she saw Rachel and Kirsty. She was wearing a black wetsuit with pink sleeves and legs, and her turquoise board had yellow edging, decorated with pink waves.

"Yes!" she said with a wide smile. "I was hoping you'd come out here for a quick surf before the competition. I'm Layne the Surfing Fairy, by the way. Queen Titania sent me to find you."

"Oh, why?" asked Kirsty, exchanging a worried look with Rachel. "Is everything OK, Layne?"

"Everything's fine," said Layne. "The queen asked me to invite you to the Fairyland Surfing Festival. Come and join in the fun."

The girls felt excitement surging through them. They knew that no time would pass in the human world while they were in Fairyland.

"We'd love to," said Rachel. "When does it start?"

"Right now," said Layne.

She winked at them and dipped her wand into the water. Silver sparkles skittered towards Rachel and Kirsty, and they and their surfboards instantly shrank to fairy size. Their filmy wings unfurled as a wave swelled up, tipped with rainbow-coloured flecks. It lifted the surfboards, and Layne popped up on to

her feet. Rachel and Kirsty did the same,
and rode through glittering spray until
they slid on to white sand.

"We're not in Port Pearl any more,"
said Kirsty with a smile.

The beach was crowded with fairies
carrying surfboards and body boards
under their arms. There were little craft
and snack stalls lined up along the sand.

Ellie the Guitar Fairy was playing a simple sea shanty beside the rock pools, and Padma the Pirate Fairy was singing along.

"This is awesome," said Rachel, waving to a few fairies that she recognised.

"Welcome to our first Surfing Festival," said Layne. "Come on, I want to show you everything."

She guided them around the different stalls. They were filled with beautiful crafts, from shell ornaments and mother-of-pearl earrings to jewelled mermaid's purses and driftwood mirrors. There was a refreshment stall giving out yummy food, and a push-along market barrow serving pop and smoothies in every colour of the rainbow. Feeling peckish, they tried crispy seaweed snacks, watermelon slices, starfish-shaped biscuits and seafoam smoothies. Ellie's music filled the air, together with the splash of the waves and the laughter of the fairies.

"Yum," said Rachel, lying back on the sand. "This is heavenly."

Just then, three surfboards slid on to the shore beside them. Layne jumped up.

"Awesome!" she exclaimed. "Rachel

and Kirsty, these are the other Gold
Medal Games Fairies – Riley the
Skateboarding Fairy, Soraya the Skiing
Fairy and Jayda the Snowboarding Fairy.
Each of us watches over one of the Gold
Medal sports."

"This is a great festival, Layne," said
Soraya. "I've been enjoying learning how
to surf."

"All thanks
to my magical
surfboard," said
Layne, hugging
it as if it were a
friend.

"It's a bit like
snowboarding,"
Jayda added.
"Only warmer!"

They all
laughed, and
Rachel and
Kirsty got to their feet.

"Rachel and Kirsty are taking part in
the Gold Medal Games," said Layne.

"Cool," said Riley, grinning at them.
"It's the skateboarding championships
tomorrow – I'll look out for you."

"Hey, what's all that commotion?" asked Soraya suddenly.

She shaded her eyes and looked over to the snack stall, where Daisy the Festival Fairy had let out a cry of surprise. Loud, angry voices drowned out the sound of the music, and the fairies beside the stall were barged out of the way.

"Oh no," said Rachel.

Jack Frost swaggered down the beach, and three goblins scrambled after him. They were all carrying surfboards. Rachel, Kirsty and the Gold Medal Games Fairies watched as they paddled out on their boards. The goblins fell off several times. Jack Frost roughly bumped other surfers out of his way. Then a wave rolled in, and he lost his balance. He was swept into the shallows and sat up crossly.

"What are you staring at, you annoying little pests?" he snapped at Rachel and Kirsty.

"Hey, that's rude," said Layne, stepping forward.

"It's none of your business," Jack Frost snapped at her.

"Actually, it *is* my business," said Layne, folding her arms across her chest. "It's my job to look after surfers everywhere. I make sure they are safe, skilful and relaxed, and that they keep up the spirit of the sport. You're spoiling the happy atmosphere of this festival. Surfing is about sharing and including, not shoving others out of the way."

Jack Frost's eyes narrowed and he pointed a long finger at Layne.

"Surfing is about winning," he hissed.

"This festival is meant for everyone," said Layne. "You are welcome to join in, but not to spoil it for everyone else. Besides, this isn't a competition and there won't be a winner. This is a festival to celebrate everything we love about surfing."

"That's stupid," said Jack Frost.

He flung down his board, and Riley fluttered nimbly out of the way.

"It's not stupid," Layne said. "It's about

sportsmanship. All the Gold Medal Games
Fairies will tell you the same thing.
Please stop shouting and join in the fun."

Jack Frost leaned towards Layne.
Rachel and Kirsty stepped up beside her.
Jack Frost was so close that they could
see tiny icicles in his stiff beard, and his
icy breath made the little hairs on their
arms stand up.

"If I can't be a winner here," he hissed,
"then I'll go somewhere I can."

Rachel and Kirsty shared a worried
glance.

"I'll win the gold medal," he went on.
"But just to make absolutely sure . . ."

Jack Frost disappeared in a flash of blue
lightning . . . and so did Layne's magical
surfboard.

Chapter Three
Lightning Jack

Layne groaned and dropped to her knees on the sand.

"This is going to ruin the festival and the Gold Medal Games," she said. "Everything will go wrong without my surfboard."

"How can we help?" Rachel asked.

Layne looked up.

"I know that you've helped many fairies before," she said. "Would you really help me?"

"Yes, of course," said Kirsty. "What would you like us to do?"

"Let's go back to Port Pearl beach," said Layne. "With your help, I might still be able to save the competition and the festival."

"We'll watch over the Surfing Festival while you're away," Jayda promised.

Layne waved her wand, and Rachel and Kirsty were whisked up in a whirl of blue and green. When the colours cleared, they were floating on their surfboards in the sea, human sized again. Layne was sitting on Kirsty's shoulder.

"Are you sure this is Port Pearl?" said

Kirsty. "It looks
very different
from when
we left."

Thick,
grey
clouds had
hidden the
sun and there
was a chill in the

air. There were a few other surfers in
the water, and they didn't sound very
friendly.

"Our school is definitely going to win,"
one girl was saying in a boastful voice.
"You might as well go home."

She scowled at a boy nearby, and he
stuck out his tongue at her.

"I think that the missing magical

surfboard is already having an effect,"
said Kirsty.

"Yes, its magic is very powerful," said
Layne. "Without it, everything that can
go wrong *will* go wrong."

A wave swelled, and everyone promptly
fell off their surfboard.

"PAH!" said Kirsty, spluttering seawater
and pulling herself back on to her board.

"That wasn't even a proper wave. Why did we all fall in?"

"Because of my missing surfboard," said Layne. "We have to find Jack Frost before the competition turns into a disaster."

She tucked herself under Kirsty's hair and they paddled back to the shore. Kensa was standing among a crowd of people who were all talking at once.

"Where's my surfboard?"

"You've given me the wrong number!"

"My name *must* be on the list!"

Two boys from different schools were shouting at each other nearby, and at that moment the judges' table collapsed.

"Oh no, whatever next?" Kensa exclaimed.

The girls checked the boards that listed who was in which heat.

"We're not in the first heat," said Rachel. "Phew, that gives us a chance to find Jack Frost."

Kensa tapped her microphone.

"Will the first competitors in this year's Gold Medal Games please enter the water," she said. "Good luck, everyone!"

Three young surfers waded into the water.

"Look, there's Shanti," said Rachel. "Good luck!"

Shanti waved to them as she paddled out.

"Who is the fourth surfer?" said Kirsty.

"Make way for the winner," shouted a scratchy voice. "Say hello to your champion, Lightning Jack!"

The girls turned and saw a sour-faced surfer in a blue wetsuit, decorated with

lightning bolts.

"I don't remember seeing him before," said Rachel.

"He looks sort of familiar . . ." said Kirsty.

Layne gasped. "That's *my* surfboard," she cried in dismay. "Lightning Jack is Jack Frost!"

He strode into the water, waving to the photographers. His spiky hair was swept back from his head, with turquoise beads plaited into it. A surfboard-shaped pendant hung around his neck.

"He's going to spoil the Gold Medal Games for everyone," said Layne. "And there's nothing I can do to stop him."

Chapter Four
Shark Surprise

Shanti was the first surfer to catch a wave. She popped up, twisted sideways . . . and flipped head over heels.

"Shanti's usually better than that," said Rachel.

Suddenly, screams came from the sea, and Kensa jumped up to the wooden

lifeguard platform.

"Sharks!" she exclaimed.

She pointed to where several dark fins had appeared in the water. Two of the surfers paddled quickly towards the shore and scrambled out of the water. Only Lightning Jack stayed still, a mean smile on his lips.

"Why isn't he worried?" asked Rachel.

The fins rose into the air and the girls gasped.

"Those aren't sharks," said Kirsty. "It's a trick. They're goblins!"

The three goblins squawked with laughter at the panic they had caused. They lifted their fin-shaped hats and waved at the audience on the beach.

"That's naughty and mean," said Layne, shaking her head.

The goblins swam away, and then
Lightning Jack caught a wave. The
audience cheered as he sped along,
keeping his balance perfectly.

"What an unforgettable performance
from Lightning Jack," gushed a nearby
reporter into her camera.

The competitors paddled out again,
and all of them managed to catch a few
waves. Shanti did better than before, but

only Lightning Jack achieved top marks
for every wave he caught. Rachel, Kirsty
and Layne could hardly bear to watch,
knowing that he was a cheat.

"What a great opening to the Gold
Medal Games," said Kensa, when the
heat was over. "Lightning Jack is going to
be hard to beat!"

The girls saw Lightning Jack walk
towards the beach café with Layne's
surfboard tucked under his arm.

"Let's follow him," said Kirsty, standing
up. "Maybe we'll get a chance to take
the magical surfboard back."

Outside the café, Lightning Jack was at
a table with three surfers. They were all
wearing green wetsuits, beanie hats and
enormous sunglasses that covered most of
their faces.

"Goblins," said Rachel at once. "I bet they're the ones who played the shark trick."

"Get me a milkshake," Lightning Jack demanded.

"Give us chips and fizzy pop," the goblins shouted. "Now!

The café staff raised their eyebrows.

"They are so rude," said Layne. "Behaviour like that is the opposite of the surfing spirit."

Lightning Jack was holding tightly to the magic surfboard. A teenage boy came up and patted him on the back.

"Wow, you were awesome," he said to Jack. "That was amazing surfing."

A young couple came up to shake his hand, praising his skills. Lightning Jack stroked his hair and slurped his milkshake.

"I've surfed much bigger waves than that," he boasted. "Soon the whole world will be talking about me. I'll be the most famous surfer of all time."

There was a cheer from the beach, and Kensa's voice rang out again.

"That was a good heat, but no one has matched Lightning Jack's awesome scores. What will the next heat bring? Those in the third heat, it's time to catch a wave!"

"That's going to spoil the competition for everyone else," said Rachel. "It's supposed to be for beginners only, but it sounds as if he's made himself unbeatable."

"I've got an idea," said Kirsty. "Maybe

if he thinks we're superfans, he'll let us look after his surfboard."

She took Rachel's hand and pushed through the growing crowd of admirers. Then she stood behind Lightning Jack and whispered into his ear.

"You're incredible, Lightning Jack," she said. "Can we do anything for you?"

"We could get you a milkshake," said Rachel into his other ear.

"Got one," Lightning Jack snapped.

"You must be tired," said Kirsty. "That

surfboard looks heavy. We could take care of it for you."

Lightning Jack waved them away without turning to look at them.

"No one touches it but me," he muttered. "Go away."

One of the goblins threw a chip at Kirsty, and another squirted tomato sauce into someone else's drink. It was chaos.

"This isn't working, and we're in the next heat," Rachel whispered, squeezing Kirsty's hand. "We have to go."

Chapter Five
Wipeout

Soon, the girls were in the sea, waiting for their first wave.

"I feel guilty for joining in when we still haven't stopped Lightning Jack," said Rachel.

Layne peeped out from under Kirsty's dark hair.

"It's important to take part and not let your schools down," she said. "Besides, surfing always helps me to focus my thoughts. Maybe it will give one of us a brainwave."

A wave swelled behind them and they started paddling. Rachel and the other surfers were too slow, but Kirsty was in just the right place. She popped up and caught the wave perfectly.

"Yes!" Rachel shouted as she saw her best friend taking off.

But suddenly, all the lessons that Kirsty had been taught flew out of her head. She looked at the wall of water, panicked and flipped off her board. Spluttering and coughing, she rose out of the water.

"Layne?" she cried, as soon as she could speak. "Layne, are you OK?"

"Here," said Layne, lowering herself on to Kirsty's shoulder. "I tied myself into your hair. It takes more than a wipeout to worry me. What happened?"

"Sorry," said Kirsty, laughing. "I started thinking about what I was doing, and suddenly it seemed impossible. And then it *was* impossible."

"You lost your confidence," said Layne. "Never mind, Kirsty. Paddle back out and try again."

"Don't worry, I'm not giving up," said Kirsty, smiling.

She paddled back towards the line-up of other surfers. The sea was calm, and they had to wait. Kirsty knew that she was at the back of the queue. Now that she had ridden a wave, it was good surfing manners to take turns.

Just when it seemed as if the sea had fallen calm, another wave swelled up. Rachel paddled for it and popped up, but the nose of the board shot upwards and she went headfirst into the water.

"Oh my goodness, are you OK?" asked Kirsty.

"I'm fine," said Rachel. "I just couldn't remember anything I'd learned."

"My magical surfboard should be helping you," said Layne, looking upset. "The waves are perfect, but everyone is losing focus and confidence."

It was the same for all the surfers in the first heats. Everyone made silly mistakes and missed their chances. When the first heats ended, all the surfers were feeling disappointed. Everyone except Lightning Jack. Rachel and Kirsty were just buying a wrap from the snack stall when they saw him sauntering past the other competitors. The goblins were scurrying after him.

"You might as well all go home," he said to the other surfers. "Did you see my marks? I got a ten from every judge. I was perfect. None of you has a chance of beating me."

"What a boaster," said Shanti, who was standing nearby.

"Let's move away from him," said another girl. "He's not very kind."

Soon, almost everyone had gone to sit on another part of the beach. Lightning Jack scowled at them with his arms folded across his chest.

"They're just jealous," he said.

"No," said Kirsty. "They don't want to be around someone who says mean, horrible things all the time."

"I know more about surfing than they ever will," Lightning Jack retorted.

"My surfboard has given you the skills of the sport," said Layne, "but you know nothing about the spirit of surfing."

Lightning Jack's face went purple with fury.

"I'm the best surfer in the world!" he exploded.

"No, you're not," said Layne. "You're not a surfer in here."

She held her hand over her heart.

"You might get a perfect ten every time you catch a wave," she said. "You might win all the competitions. But you won't be a true surfer if *all* you care about is winning. All the Gold Medal

Games Fairies would agree with me. The feeling you get when you ride the perfect wave – that's what it's all about."

"Winning is all that matters!" Lightning Jack yelled. "I'm going to be the best and the most famous. Who cares about feelings?"

"We care," said Kirsty, taking a step forward.

Lightning Jack yanked his wand out from inside his wetsuit.

"Fine," he

said. "Goblins, go and steal *all* the Gold
Medal Games Fairies' magical objects.
Let's see how much humans care about
the sports when they can't win."

"Wait, no!" cried Rachel.

The goblins vanished with a wave
of Lightning Jack's wand, and the girls
shared a horrified glance. Lightning Jack
was going to spoil all the Gold Medal
Games!

Chapter Six
Dominoes

Cackling with laughter, Lightning Jack
stomped off towards the photographers.
All the competitors were lining up for
a group photo. Most of the surfers had
stuck their boards into the sand.

"They look like a row of dominoes,"
said Rachel.

"I've got an idea," exclaimed Kirsty. "But I need Lightning Jack to stick the magical surfboard in the sand. Layne, could you magic up a camera?"

Layne waved her wand, and suddenly Rachel was holding an enormous camera.

"If you can make him put the surfboard with the others, I'll start the best game of dominoes ever," said Kirsty with a grin.

Rachel hurried towards Lightning Jack, holding the camera up to her face so he didn't recognise her. Kirsty stayed behind him, out of sight.

"Let me see the star of the games,"
Rachel called to him.

Lightning Jack pouted and posed with
his board.

"Just pop the board to the side, please,"
Rachel called out. "I'd like a close-up for
our cover."

Lightning Jack jammed the board into
the sand with the others, but stayed right
next to it.

"Just a little closer to me," said Rachel. "Closer . . . closer . . ."

Lightning Jack took one step away from the board.

"Now!" Rachel yelled, dropping the camera.

"I know you!" Lightning Jack exclaimed.

He whirled around, just in time to see Kirsty push the board at the end of the row. All the surfboards went down like dominoes.

"No!" yelled Lightning Jack.

It was pandemonium. Surfers piled on top of each other, trying to find their boards. Arms and legs flailed around, and the girls fell to their hands and knees, searching through the jumble of boards.

"Could our first four competitors

please take their positions for the second round of heats," said Kensa through the microphone.

"Somebody find my board!" Lightning Jack screamed at the remaining surfers.

"It doesn't work like that, friend," said another surfer, patting him on the back.

"You're not the boss."

"I'm getting really fed up with this surfing spirit," hissed Lightning Jack.

Just then, Rachel saw a flash of turquoise at the bottom of the pile.

"There!" she cried, pointing.

Layne slid down a lock of Kirsty's hair and landed on the magical surfboard. As soon as her feet touched it, the board shrank to

fairy size. Layne picked it
up and zoomed into
Rachel's pocket.
It was so frantic
that no one had
noticed her.
No one except
Lightning
Jack. He glared
at Rachel and
Kirsty.

"You're those pests
who help the fairies," he said with a
scowl. "You'll be sorry for this!"

He turned and stomped away, yanking
the beads out of his hair as he went.

"Now that I have my board back, I can
make sure that no one will remember
he was here," said Layne, fluttering

out of Rachel's pocket. "But I must go back to the festival now. Good luck in the competition, and thank you for everything. Today would have been a disaster without you."

"I hope that the goblins didn't manage to steal the other magical objects," Rachel said.

"If they did, we might need your help again," said Layne.

"Any time!" said the girls together.

Layne raised her hand in a final wave. Then she flicked her wand and vanished in a flurry of sparkles.

Instantly, sunlight streamed on to the beach and the grey clouds scudded away. The crowd burst into cheers as Shanti caught her first wave and surfed the barrel all the way to shore.

"Yes!" Rachel cheered, jumping up and down. "That's more like it!"

The afternoon was a haze of sunshine, surfing and sea spray. By the time the two highest scorers paddled into the water for the final heat, Rachel and Kirsty had almost forgotten that it was a competition. Shanti was one of the finalists, and the girls cheered her until their throats were hoarse.

"I can't believe how quickly today has gone," said Rachel, as Shanti waded out of the water for the last time.

The sun was dipping towards the horizon, and the girls lay back on the warm sand feeling tired and happy.

"Time always seems to go extra fast on the beach," said Kirsty.

The microphone whined and the girls sat up. Kensa was standing at the front of the little wooden stage.

"The results are in," she announced. "What a fantastic day! After a shaky start, everyone put in an amazing effort. When I remember that you're beginners and you only started learning a few weeks ago, I think you are all winners."

There was a huge round of applause. Kensa grinned and waited for everyone

to settle down.

"However, there can only be one gold medallist," she went on. "So it gives me great pleasure to award this year's Surfing Gold Medal to . . . Shanti Sharma of Tippington School!"

The crowd cheered and whooped, and Rachel and her schoolfriends went crazy with excitement. Beaming happily, Shanti walked up to collect her award.

"The Gold Medal Games will continue tomorrow with our skateboarding championship," said Kensa. "I hope we'll see you all there."

Rachel and Kirsty picked up their surfboards.

"I wonder if the goblins managed to steal the other magical items, and what they were," said Rachel.

"I have a feeling that our next fairy adventure is just around the corner," Kirsty said. "But right now, I think it's time for a sunset surfing session. Race you to the next wave!"

The End

Now it's time for Kirsty and Rachel to help...

Riley the Skateboarding Fairy

Read on for a sneak peek...

"Where am I?"

For a moment, when Rachel Walker opened her eyes, she was confused. Then she heard the distant *shush-shush* of the waves on the shore, and the strident squawk of seagulls. Of course! She was in the pretty seaside town of Port Pearl, where she and her school friends were taking part in the Gold Medal Games, the biggest schools' sports competition in the country. Luckily, her best friend Kirsty Tate's school was competing too, so they could enjoy the fun together.

"Yesterday was the best," Rachel

whispered with a smile.

She sat up and looked around the youth hostel dormitory that she was sharing with her classmates. They were all fast asleep. A large gold medal was hanging on the end of Shanti Sharma's bed. Shanti had won the surfing competition yesterday, and everyone from Tippington School was very proud of her.

Today was the skateboarding competition, and Rachel was already feeling too excited to go back to sleep.

She slipped out of bed and quietly pulled on her shorts and T-shirt. She felt sure that Kirsty would already be down by the sea. After checking with her teacher, she headed down to the beach behind the hostel. Sure enough, her best friend was paddling in the shallows.

"Isn't this gorgeous?" Kirsty said, twirling around with her arms stretched out. "I couldn't stay in bed a minute longer."

Rachel pulled off her sandals and waded into the cool water.

Read Riley the Skateboarding Fairy to find out what adventures are in store for Kirsty and Rachel!

Read the brand-new series from Daisy Meadows…

Unicorn Magic™

Ride. Dream. Believe.

Meet best friends Aisha and Emily and journey to the secret world of Enchanted Valley!

Calling all parents, carers and teachers!
The Rainbow Magic fairies are here to help
your child enter the magical world of reading.
Whatever reading stage they are at, there's
a Rainbow Magic book for everyone!
Here is Lydia the Reading Fairy's guide to
supporting your child's journey at all levels.

Starting Out

Our Rainbow Magic Beginner Readers are perfect for first-time readers who are just beginning to develop reading skills and confidence. Approved by teachers, they contain a full range of educational levelling, as well as lively full-colour illustrations.

1

Developing Readers

Rainbow Magic Early Readers contain longer stories and wider vocabulary for building stamina and growing confidence. These are adaptations of our most popular Rainbow Magic stories, specially developed for younger readers in conjunction with an Early Years reading consultant, with full-colour illustrations.

2

Going Solo

The Rainbow Magic chapter books - a mixture of series and one-off specials - contain accessible writing to encourage your child to venture into reading independently. These highly collectible and much-loved magical stories inspire a love of reading to last a lifetime.

3

www.orchardseriesbooks.co.uk

"Rainbow Magic got my daughter reading chapter books. Great sparkly covers, cute fairies and traditional stories full of magic that she found impossible to put down" - Mother of Edie (6 years)

"Florence LOVES the Rainbow Magic books. She really enjoys reading now" - Mother of Florence (6 years)

Read along the Reading Rainbow!

Well done – you have completed the book!

This book was worth 1 star.

See how far you have climbed on the Reading Rainbow opposite.
The more books you read, the more stars you can colour in
and the closer you will be to becoming a Royal Fairy!

Do you want to print your own Reading Rainbow?

1) Go to the Rainbow Magic website

2) Download and print out the poster

3) Colour in a star for every book you finish
and climb the Reading Rainbow

4) For every step up the rainbow,
you can download your very own certificate

There's all this and lots more at
orchardseriesbooks.co.uk

You'll find activities, stories, a special newsletter
AND you can search for the fairy with your name!